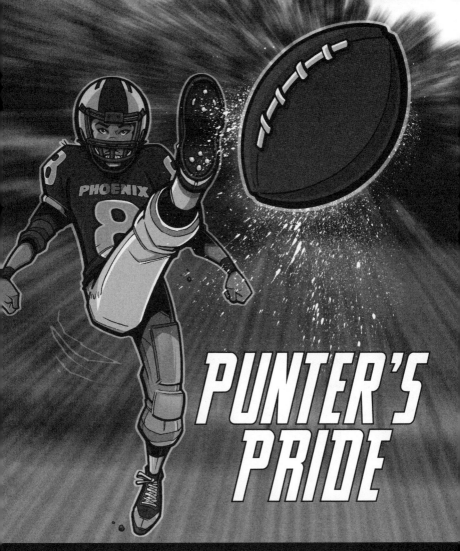

PUNTER'S PRIDE

BY JAKE MADDOX

Text by Tyler Omoth
Illustrated by Sean Tiffany

STONE ARCH BOOKS
a capstone imprint

Jake Maddox Sports Stories are published by
Stone Arch Books
a Capstone Imprint
1710 Roe Crest Drive
North Mankato, Minnesota 56003

www.mycapstone.com

Library of Congress Cataloguing-in-Publication Data is available on the Library of
Congress website.

ISBN: 978-1-4965-4956-3 (library binding)
ISBN: 978-1-4965-4958-7 (paperback)
ISBN: 978-1-4965-4960-0 (eBook PDF)

Summary: Nolan is running for class president and is also the punter for
the school's undefeated football team. But when injuries force him into a the
quarterback position, it's a lot to handle all at once.

Editor: Nate LeBoutillier
Designer: Lori Bye
Production Specialist: Tori Abraham

Printed in Canada.
010382F17

TABLE OF CONTENTS

CHAPTER 1

PRACTICE PERFECT

Coach Lewis blew his whistle. He yelled, "Punt formation!"

As Nolan ran out onto the Phoenix's practice field, Tony stuck his foot out to trip him. Nolan jumped over the outstretched foot easily.

"Punters aren't real football players!" Tony said. "The last thing we need is for a punter to goof up our perfect season with only two games to go."

"Linebackers are too slow," said Nolan. "Even the good ones. You do your part, and I'll do mine.

The Phoenix's special teams units lined up for the punt. Nolan took his spot 13 yards behind the line of scrimmage.

At center, Luis looked back through his own legs as he prepared to snap the ball. As a fellow special teams player, Luis was Nolan's good friend — and a very reliable long snapper.

"Right into my hands, Luis," Nolan said.

When Nolan gave the signal, Luis shot the ball through his legs in a perfect spiral. Nolan nabbed the ball, held it with outstretched arms, and took two quick steps forward. On the third step, he dropped the ball.

Boom!

Nolan sent the ball flying with a hard kick. The ball flew to the other side of the practice field. By the time it came down out of the sky, players from the punting unit had already collected under it and were waiting to tackle. The punt returner waived one hand in the air to signal a fair catch and caught the ball on the six-yard line.

"Great punt, Nolan!" said Coach Lewis.

"Yeah, whatever," grumbled Tony. "It's easy to kick the short ones. Out-kick your coverage, and he'll run it back all the way!"

Nolan looked at Coach Lewis. The coach looked back at him and winked.

"All right," Coach Lewis yelled. "Let's back it up 30 yards and do it again."

The special teams units lined up again. This time there was no way Nolan could pin the return man against the end zone. He would have to punt the ball as far as he could and also high enough to give his teammates a chance to make the tackle.

Nolan gave the signal and once again the ball zoomed from Luis's crouched position into Nolan's hands. From the corner of his eye, Nolan could see Tony rushing around the edge. He was running directly for Nolan and wore a hungry and slightly scary expression behind his facemask.

Nolan took two strong steps to build up his power and dropped the ball.

Boom!

Nolan gave the kick everything he had. The football flew past the outstretched hands of Tony, who dove to block the punt. The football sailed so far that the return man had to run backward to get underneath it. He caught it and started to run it back. But he made it only five yards before Nolan's teammates wrapped him up around the ankles and brought him down.

Nolan looked down at Tony and extended a hand to help Tony up. After all, they were teammates. "Better luck next time," Nolan said.

Tony ignored Nolan's hand and rose to his feet. "I *will* get it next time," he replied.

A cheer went up from the sideline. Holding a sign that said *Punter for President!* was a kid wearing glasses and an Albert Einstein shirt.

Luis looked at Nolan. "What's that about?"

"I'm running for class president," Nolan said. "Quincy's my campaign manager. He said he wants to watch practice to see what football skills of mine might translate to the campaign."

"Isn't he the president of the math club?" asked Luis.

"Yeah," said Nolan. "And the debate team."

"Valuable guy," said Luis.

"I still could use a vice president," said Nolan. "What do you say? I already depend on you."

Luis's eyes widened. "Me? What do I know about, like, politics or whatever?"

"You can learn anything you don't know," said Nolan.

Luis looked over at Quincy, who had put down his sign and picked up a book to read.

"Would I have to give any speeches?" asked Luis. "I'm terrible at speeches. I get nervous."

Nolan laughed and said, "I'll take care of that. I just need you to support me and make me look good. I could use a little muscle on my side."

Luis looked around like someone was watching. When he seemed satisfied that no one was, he said quietly, "Why not?"

CHAPTER 2

GAME TIME

Nolan put on his helmet and paced up and down the sideline.

The Phoenix were down, 20-17, and it was already the fourth quarter. The offense was at midfield but hadn't scored in the second half. It was an ugly third down with nine yards to go. Nolan had punted the last four possessions in a row and was ready for another should the offense not pick up the first down.

"Come on, guys!" Coach Lewis yelled. "You know the play. Now execute!"

Nolan stopped his pacing to look over at Luis, who was watching the game with his helmet tucked under his arm.

"You've got to cool it," Luis said to Nolan.

"Why's that?" said Nolan.

"To show a little confidence in Jamaal," said Luis. "He's the best quarterback in the conference. He'll get this."

The third down play was a quick slant pass, but the defense covered it up right away. A quick tackle meant the Phoenix only gained two yards.

Coach Lewis called for the punting unit and beckoned Nolan. Nolan bolted over to Coach Lewis's side.

"Try and pin them back by hitting the right corner down by the goal line," he said. "We need a good one. We're running out of time."

Nolan, Luis, and the rest of the punting unit ran out to the field. Behind him, Nolan heard Tony yell, "Don't blow it!"

As they lined up for the play, Nolan looked around to assess the situation. *Okay,* he thought.

We're at the 45-yard line on their side of midfield. I need to go high and aim for that corner. We can't afford to let them run it back.

"Hike!"

Luis's snap sailed into Nolan's hands. Nolan caught the ball and quickly spun it so the laces were on the top. He took two quick steps and let his right leg fly back and snap forward like a cracking whip.

Boom!

The football shot through the air, spiraling inside the ten and just short of the goal line. Nolan's teammates raced down field to tackle the return man, but there was no need. The ball landed on the four-yard line and bounced to the right, directly out of bounds. The referees blew their whistles and marked the spot.

Luis ran up and popped Nolan on the shoulder pads. "Great punt!" said Luis.

14

Nolan jogged back to the sideline with a grin on his face. Up in the stands, Quincy smiled and held high his sign: *Punter for President.* Quincy sat among a circle of other math club and debate team students he'd enlisted to come to the game to support Nolan. Nolan smiled and gave a quick thumbs up to his cheering section.

As the defense took the field, Nolan spotted Tony. "Stop 'em!" he said.

Tony scowled. But he and the Phoenix D stuffed two run plays in a row. Then Tony batted down a pass on third and long, forcing a punt. It was a good punt. The Phoenix again had the ball at midfield. But now there were only 23 seconds left on the clock.

On the first play, Jamaal tossed a quick pass to Caden, the team's top receiver. Caden ran for the sideline but was tackled before he could cross it. The clock continued to run.

"Time out!" Jamaal yelled to the referees.

The refs blew their whistles and stopped the clock with just seven ticks left.

Jamaal ran over to the sideline to talk to Coach Lewis. Nolan moved closer, so he could hear the discussion.

"What do you think?" Coach Lewis asked. "They're going to have everyone back. If we throw it to the end zone, do you think that Caden can outjump them?"

Jamaal shrugged. "Maybe," he said, "but I have a better idea. They'll be completely ignoring our running backs. What if we send the receivers and tight ends down the field as decoys and then dump it off to T.J. in the flat? If he needs to lateral, I'll follow him."

Coach Lewis looked at T.J., the team's running back. T.J. didn't say anything. T.J. rarely said anything. He just liked to get the ball, put his head down, and run.

Coach Lewis smiled and nodded. "Great idea. Go do it!"

Jamaal put his helmet on as he ran back out onto the field. He called the play, broke the huddle, and stepped up to the line of scrimmage. He took the snap and backpedaled. As the receivers sprinted down the field, the defenders followed them.

Suddenly, a defensive end ripped past his blocker and was headed for Jamaal's blind side. T.J. had broken free out of the backfield and was wide open in the flat. Jamaal drew his arm back and fired a laser to him just before the defensive end hit.

Crack!

Nolan heard the crowd cheering and screaming as T.J. took the ball down the field, but Nolan wasn't watching T.J. He didn't see T.J. dodge each tackler and stiff-arm the strong safety.

Nolan didn't see the T.J.'s amazing and desperate dive into the end zone to win the game. Though the crowd went wild, Nolan focused on the Phoenix backfield.

Jamaal was down, and he looked like he was hurt badly.

CHAPTER 3

MIDFIELD CAMPAIGN

The next day at practice, Nolan edged in next to Caden and Jamaal as Coach Lewis called the team together at midfield.

The whole team stopped talking and kneeled on the grass to listen. Coach Lewis had something to say. By the look on his face, it wasn't good.

"That was a great win yesterday," Coach Lewis said. The Phoenix are still undefeated."

Despite his words, nobody cheered. They were waiting to hear what Coach Lewis would say next.

"I think most of you know that Jamaal took a pretty hard shot there at the end of the game," Coach Lewis said.

"A dirty shot," said Tony.

"No, Tony," Coach Lewis said. "I've seen a replay on video, and it wasn't dirty. It was a clean hit. Unfortunately, Jamaal's head smashed into the ground after the hit. He has a concussion. With just one game left, he's done for the season."

Groans, sighs, and other sounds of frustration echoed through the group.

Coach Lewis held up a hand to quiet them. "That's the bad news," he said. "The good news is that we have the best second-string quarterback in the conference. Believe me when I tell you that Van could be the starting QB for any other team out there. So we're going to have a light practice today in terms of hitting. But we need to run through a lot of offensive sets. I want Van to get serious reps with the first team offense."

Nolan cleared his throat.

"Oh yeah," Coach Lewis said. "Before we head out, Nolan would like to say something."

Nolan stood up and faced the team. His hands started to shake a little, but he grabbed his helmet with both hands and held it in front of him to cover up. "Hi, guys," said Nolan. "As some of you know, I'm running for class president this year."

The team razzed him and shouted a bunch of stuff at him. He ducked as a towel flew past his head. He smiled and noticed that most of the guys had smiles on their faces, too. They were just giving him a hard time.

Tony did not have a smile on his face. "You can't have a punter for president!" he said.

"Why's that?" Nolan said.

"Let's see," Tony said, "punters barely do a thing. They don't throw or run or tackle. Well, okay, maybe on a trick play. Or a messed-up play. They're only on the team as last resorts."

A defensive end chimed in. "Yeah, who wants a last resort as class president?"

Nolan's hands began to shake again, but he forced himself to smile. "Hold on a minute," he said. "Let's take a closer look." He cracked his knuckles and began to pace in front of his teammates.

Luis pursed his lips. When Nolan looked at him, Luis raised his eyebrows as if to say, *Well, what* do *punters do?*

"What exactly *do* punters do?" said Nolan. "Well, let me tell you what punters do. When the team is in trouble, they come in to fix things. As you mentioned, punters actually *do* pass, run, or tackle on occasion. And more importantly, they can be vital in winning the field position part of the game. As class president, I'll do the same thing. Where I see problems, I'll step in and try to help the students improve their position."

Tony snickered and said, "Punters can't even get into the Hall of Fame!"

"Not true," Nolan said. "Ray Guy was inducted into the Pro Football Hall of Fame in 2014. He averaged over forty yards per punt and played in three Super Bowls with the Raiders. He helped his team win."

A couple guys looked at each other.

"If Ray Guy is worthy of a Hall of Fame vote," said Nolan, "you guys can vote for me!"

Luis jumped up. "Punter for president!"

The rest of the team laughed, and many joined in the chant of "Punter for president! Punter for president!"

Nolan shifted his helmet to his left hand and began shaking hands with teammates with his right.

CHAPTER 4

NEXT MAN UP

"All right. That's enough campaigning," Coach Lewis said. "Let's get to practice. First team offense and first team defense, take the field. Van, it's your show."

Nolan and Luis stood by as the first team offense and defense took the field. They ran through a couple simple plays. On the third play, Van faked the handoff and bootlegged out to his left. With Tony chasing after him, he threw a pass to Caden coming across the middle. It was right on target.

"He passes the ball about as well as Jamaal," Luis said.

"Yeah, and he might run the ball even better," Nolan said.

Coach Lewis blew his whistle. "Great job, guys. Van, nice throw, but did you see how open the field was down the sideline? Don't be afraid to take it yourself. You have the speed to pick up the first down. Okay, let's try it again."

The offense and defense lined up again. This time Van took the snap, faked the handoff going to the left, and spun back to the right. Like a shot, he took off down the sideline. The whole defense bit on the fake handoff except for Tony.

Van ran for the sideline and then turned upfield. Just before Tony wrapped his arms around him, Van took one last lunging step forward to escape Tony's grasp.

Tony held on as Van crumbled and let out a cry of agony.

Tony popped up. "I didn't do it!" he said.

Van was still on the ground with both hands clutching the back of his thigh.

Van had clearly just pulled his hamstring muscle. It was a common injury, but one that healed slowly.

What luck, thought Nolan. *The Phoenix are cursed at quarterback.*

While Coach Lewis and a trainer tended to Van, the rest of the team gathered nearby.

"Great," said Tony. "Now what?"

"Do we even have a third string quarterback?" asked Caden.

"I guess we're going to find out," Luis said.

After a few minutes, Coach Lewis and the trainer helped Van get up and handed him off to a couple of the offensive linemen.

"Pair up, grab a ball, and start playing catch," said Coach Lewis. "Start at ten yards distance apart."

The team manager unzipped a bag of balls and tossed them to the team.

Nolan grabbed a ball and jogged out on to the field with Luis close behind. They started playing catch, throwing the ball easily back and forth. Luis's throws were wobbly but still easy enough to catch. Nolan lobbed lazy spirals back.

After a few minutes, Coach Lewis spoke up again. "Okay, back it up another ten yards."

With 20 yards in between them, it was harder for Luis to get the ball accurately to Nolan. But Nolan's passes were tight and on-target. Up and down the line, some balls flew wide or over the heads of their intended targets, sending guys running. It quickly became quite clear who could throw and who could not.

"Hold up," Coach Lewis said. "Caden, Tony, and Nolan. Form a triangle 30 yards apart."

Each of the three threw a number of on-the-money spirals. Caden was clearly the best, but Tony and Nolan were almost as good.

"That settles it," Coach Lewis said. "I think I've found our next man up. Good job, Tony, but keep your focus on defense. Caden, you looked good, but we need your skills at wide receiver. Nolan, you've just been elected quarterback."

The football Nolan was holding dropped at the same time as his jaw. As Luis came over to give him a high-five, Nolan tried to speak but couldn't. When he found his voice, finally, all he could say was, "Quarterback? *Me?* Me? *Quarterback?*"

Coach Lewis laughed. "You're a smart kid, Nolan. You'll do fine."

CHAPTER 5

PARK PRACTICE

Later at the city park, Nolan, T.J., and Luis gathered around a picnic table. They watched as Caden scribbled out Xs and Os and arrows on a pad of paper. For a good half an hour, Caden scribbled and talked the group through plays. Nolan recognized many of the plays, having seen them in live action on the field. But seeing them on paper was different. More like schoolwork than football.

"What do you think?" said Caden.

"It's a lot to think about," Nolan said.

"Now what?" said Luis. "Why did you want us to meet over here at the park? We could've studied plays at my kitchen table. Over cookies and milk."

Caden tossed a football to Luis. "Because now we need to practice," Caden said.

"But we were just at practice a couple of hours ago," Luis said.

"Yeah," Nolan said, "and Luis and I still need to make campaign posters this evening. Quincy set up a meeting at seven o' clock."

"That means we still have about an hour to practice," said Caden. "And afterward, T.J. and I will help with the posters. Right T.J.?"

T.J., quiet as usual, simply nodded.

"Fair enough," said Nolan.

For the next hour, Caden played coach. He led Nolan through numerous passing plays and drills. At first, Nolan's timing was off. His passes were behind Caden and T.J., who joined in running routes. As they repeated the routes, Nolan learned just how much to lead his receiver so he could catch the ball without

breaking stride. After practicing the basics, they moved onto more complex routes.

At one point, Tony and three other members of the Phoenix defense rode up on their bikes.

"What are you guys doing?" Tony said. He laughed and smacked one of his buddies on the shoulder. "Look, guys. It's a punter trying to run an offense. We'd better be awesome on defense because we're not going to score at all."

"Are you trying to make fun of Nolan for practicing?" said Caden.

Tony scowled. "I can't wait to see you in practice tomorrow," he said. "It's going to be sack city! And, oh by the way, I'm running for class president, too. You're going to get crushed twice."

Nolan smiled.

Luis scowled. "Mess with Nolan, and I'll mess with you," he said.

Tony and his buddies laughed and rode off.

"May the best man win!" Nolan yelled after them.

"Wow," Caden said. "You handled that pretty well."

"I'd like to handle Tony," Luis said.

"Back to work," said Caden.

The boys continued their work in a rush of throwing, catching, sprinting, huffing, and puffing. As the practice wound down, Caden even showed Nolan a couple trick plays, including the flea flicker, which Nolan picked up quickly. When Caden finally called for an end to the extra practice session, the boys collapsed on the ground, totally exhausted.

"Let's not get too comfortable," Nolan said after a minute. "It's campaign poster time."

Caden and Luis and T.J. groaned.

CHAPTER 6

CLASSROOM CONFLICT

The next day during lunch hour, Nolan, Luis, and Caden went up and down the halls of their school hanging up their new posters.

Punter for President!

Nolan Knows!

Coach Lewis Trusts Him, And You Can, Too!

The last one was Caden's idea. "Hey," he said. "Coach Lewis trusts you enough to be our field general for the most important game of the season. That must count for something, you know?"

They hung up the last poster, sticking it right by the entrance to the cafeteria. Then it was time to head to the auditorium for the candidates' speeches.

As he strolled the hallway, Nolan saw Jamaal standing by his locker.

"Hey, Jamaal," Nolan said. "How are you feeling, buddy?"

"A little better," Jamaal said. "I'm still getting headaches, though."

"Bummer," said Nolan.

"Hey," said Jamaal. "I wanted to tell you not to worry too much about being under center. You're smart. You'll do fine."

"Thanks," Nolan said. "I'm nowhere near as good as you or Van, but I'm all that's left."

"I've seen you throw," Jamaal said. "You have a good arm. Just don't forget your checkdowns. If the first option isn't open downfield, hit your tight end or running back. Five yards is still a good play."

"I'll keep that in mind," Nolan said. "Hey, are you going to vote tomorrow?"

"Of course," Jamaal said. "I haven't decided who to vote for, though."

Nolan's eyes went wide. "Seriously?" he said.

Jamaal smiled and slugged Nolan in the shoulder. "I'm kidding. Quarterbacks stick together," Nolan said.

Just then a loud *thump* made Nolan jump.

Tony slammed a locker nearby. He pointed at one of Nolan's signs nearby and shook his head. "Punter for president? I don't think so," he said.

"Are you ready for your campaign speech?" asked Nolan. "The race is heating up."

"The way I see it, there's not much competition," said Tony.

"Well, I can't wait to hear what you have to say," Nolan said.

"I've got it all figured out," Tony said.

"Really?" said Nolan.

"Yep," said Tony, sneering. "When they hear what I have to say, there is no way they'll decide to punt. Punting is giving up. A punter for president is *really* giving up."

Nolan pasted on a polite smile. "Punting is not giving up," he said. "It's a wise and useful strategy."

"Strategy *schmat-egy*," said Tony. "You're going down, punter."

"I'm glad you're confident," said Nolan, "You're going to have to be at your best to beat me. I have a rock-solid platform."

"Platform *schmat-form*," said Tony. "You don't know what you're talking about."

Nolan continued to grin as Tony turned his back and walked away. Nolan knew that Tony was just a big talker, but it sort of bothered him, the stuff Tony said about punters.

Nolan walked into the auditorium and found a seat near the front. Slowly, the seats began to fill with students and chatter. Nolan closed his eyes and went over his speech mentally for a few minutes. He'd memorized the entire thing.

Quincy showed up wearing a *Punter for President* button. "How are you feeling, Nolan?" he said.

"Not bad," said Nolan. "Maybe a little nervous. Maybe a little angry."

Quincy pushed up his glasses with his pinky finger. "Angry? That doesn't sound like you. You're not letting the big linebreaker guy bother you, are you?"

"I think you mean *linebacker*," said Nolan. "And, yes, that might be the problem."

Quincy put his hand on Nolan's shoulder. "Don't worry about him," he said. "His brain is likely hamster-powered."

Nolan laughed. "You know how to break the tension, Quincy. Thanks."

Quincy smiled and took a seat. "Punter for President," he said. "Pin 'em deep."

Finally, Mrs. Moen, the social studies teacher, took the auditorium stage. She stepped behind a podium and waited for the student body to quiet down.

"The birthplace of democracy," she said into a microphone. "Who can tell me what culture I am talking about? Tony?"

Surprised to hear his name, Tony looked up. "Um . . . England?"

A couple students laughed.

"Not quite," said Mrs. Moen. "How about you, Nolan? I was wondering if at least one of our candidates knows the answer."

"Ancient Greece?" Nolan said, his voice wavering slightly. He held his breath.

"That's right," said Mrs. Moen. "And since you got the right answer, you may go first. Students, it's time for the speeches from our candidates for class president. All candidates please step up to the stage."

Nolan swallowed hard. *Punting is a lot easier than this,* he thought.

CHAPTER 7

TOE TO TOE

Nolan rose from his seat and walked onto the stage. Tony followed, slapping high-fives down the aisle as he made his way to the stage.

"Tony, who is your vice president running mate again?" Mrs. Moen asked.

"I don't actually have one yet," Tony said. "This was kind of a last minute blitz."

"Okay, but you'll want to find one to help you out if you should win," Mrs. Moen said. "Ladies and gentlemen, I now give you your class president candidates. Nolan, you have the floor."

Nolan cleared his throat. "I have a list of twenty-five items that I'd like to address," he said. "But from that list, I will share with you the three I deem most important. Number one: better lockers. How many of you have lockers that stick when you try to open them?"

The students murmured. A few hands went up in the air.

"If elected, I will talk to our principal and fix that. Number two, better technology. Our computers are outdated, right?"

A few students nodded, but it wasn't the swelling response Nolan hoped for.

"Well, if I get my way, each student will have his or her own school-provided laptop. And number three, I vow to put together a plan, along with the faculty, to raise money for field trips to visit one or more of our state's greatest landmarks. What better way to learn than to experience things for ourselves? These are the promises I vow to uphold if you will elect me to be your class president. I know how to fix problems."

When Nolan had finished, the students applauded politely.

"Very good, Nolan," Mrs. Moen said. "And now let's hear from Marin."

Marin was a shy girl, and Nolan was surprised that she was running at all. She looked as nervous as Nolan. During Marin's speech, Nolan noticed the students were giving Marin the same sort of applause they'd given him. Polite but not excited.

Nolan's thoughts drifted. He wished he could re-do his speech and infuse more energy into it. Before long, Marin's speech was over.

Mrs. Moen took center stage. "And now, for our third and final candidate, Tony."

Tony took a step forward and smiled the same smile he wore after a big sack in a football game. "Ladies and germs of the school," he said, "I have one very important word for you."

The students' laughter at his ladies and germs joke fell silent. They waited to hear what he'd say next. Tony paused, letting the silence draw out.

"Pizza," he said at last.

The entire auditorium erupted into cheers and applause. A pack of guys on the football team hooted and yelled, "Pizza! Pizza! Pizza!"

Nolan rolled his eyes.

"Pizza is on the school menu only once a month," Tony said. "If you elect me student council president, I will do everything I can to get it on the menu three times each month. That way, even if they don't give in completely, we could double our pizza with two times per month. This is my vow to you."

Tony finished with an exaggerated bow.

Tons of students stood, clapping and shouting out, "Pizza! Pizza! Pizza!"

As the students continued to cheer, Nolan looked at Tony and said, "You know you'll never be able to do that, right? They have strict standards they have to follow for the menu."

"We'll see," Tony said. "You can't do anything if you can't get elected."

Nolan looked out at the sea of students as they cheered and clapped for Tony's pizza proposal. How could Nolan's fundraising plan, which would take a lot of work and help, compete with Tony's pizza plan?

"Okay, calm down," said Mrs. Moen. "Tomorrow is election day, so make sure to make your vote count."

CHAPTER 8

PEPPERONI AND DOUBT

Back home Nolan opened the front door and was swarmed by the aroma of pizza. He tossed his backpack and football bag to the floor and started up the stairs to his bedroom.

"Nolan! Hey!" his mom said. "I made your favorite. With tomorrow being such a big day, I figured we could all pig out on pizza tonight."

"I'm not hungry," Nolan said. At the top of the stairs, he turned down the hall, entered his room, and slammed the door.

After a few minutes, there was a knock on the door.

"Hey, Superstar," said his dad from the other side of the door. "What's up?"

"Nothing," Nolan said. "Go away, please."

"I want you to let me in before I count to five. Either that or I'll just assume you're dancing in your underwear again."

Nolan stifled a chuckle. His dad always knew how to make him laugh. He got up from the bed and opened the door. His dad walked in and sat on the edge of the bed.

"Your mom tells me that you're not excited about pizza," he said. "That tipped me off that there is probably something seriously, I mean drastically, wrong."

Nolan sighed but stayed silent.

His dad sighed, too. "So, let's see, what could it be? Tomorrow is the big game, so how did your first, and only, practice as the starting quarterback go?"

Nolan shrugged. "Not too bad, I guess," he said. "Tony sacked me pretty hard, even though I had the red jersey on. He said he needed to know I could take a hit."

"Is that it?" his dad said.

"Other than that, it was okay," Nolan said. "Jonny, our center, helps me read the defense. Caden gives me tips on other stuff."

"But it's up to you to make the plays, right?"

"Yeah," Nolan said. "But I didn't ask for this! I *like* punting."

"Hmm . . . okay," his dad said. "Tomorrow is also the election, right?"

At this Nolan just threw himself down, face-first, on to the bed.

"I see," his dad said. "Talk to me."

Nolan began to speak, mostly, into his pillow. "I'm running against Tony, and his main campaign promise is to get us more pizza for lunch each month."

Nolan's dad inhaled deeply through his nose. "Well, that explains why you're not excited about dinner. What kid won't vote for pizza?"

"I know, right?" Nolan said.

"Nolan," his father said, "I want you to think about something. Someone needs to be class president, and you stepped up to take on the challenge. You even had a great plan. Then, when the team needed help, even though it's an unfamiliar position, you stepped up to take on the challenge."

"What good is that if I lose the election *and* the game?"

His dad reached out and put a hand on Nolan's shoulder.

"When your peers needed you to step up, at least you tried," he said. "Who else can say that? Besides, what if you win both? It could happen."

Nolan seriously doubted this was possible.

CHAPTER 9

GAME TIME

The last game of the season was an away game against the New Hampton Knights. It was the quietest bus ride the team had taken all season. The tension of a near-perfect season mixed with their new quarterback situation had everyone on edge.

After the bus pulled to a stop by the New Hampton field, the team filed off and went over to their side of the field. Coach Lewis gathered them together. "Listen up!" he said. "I just got a text from Principal Stone. The votes have been tallied and Tony is your new class president. Congratulations, Tony."

Tony's friends whooped and yelled. Tony just smiled and shrugged. His teammates pounded on his shoulder pads in congratulations.

Nolan tried to smile, but now his confidence was lower than ever. Caden and Luis and T.J. gave him fist bumps in consolation, but Nolan felt stung. His burning disappointment was a strange mix of embarrassment, failure, and hurt pride.

Coach Lewis quieted the team again, saying, "With that news out of the way, I have something else important to tell you. Take a step closer and put your game faces on."

The Phoenix obeyed their coach and gathered in a snug circle. Nolan looked around. Somehow, he'd gotten stuck next to Tony, and they were touching shoulder pads in the close quarters.

"I know you guys are nervous about this," said Coach Lewis. "I know that some guys might have the jitters. But remember that this must be a team effort. Look around you. We've worked hard to get here. Today, we must play hard, play together, and help each other out. Now let's go get that perfect season!"

The whole team seemed to let their nervousness go at once. They yelled and pumped their fists and hoisted their helmets above their heads. They chanted, "Phoenix! Phoenix! Phoenix!"

Half an hour of warm-ups later, the Phoenix were kicking off to the Knights, and the game was on. Nolan watched from the sideline as Tony and the defense tried to stuff the Knights' high-powered running game. But the Knights marched right down the field and into field goal territory.

On third down and eight, the Knights tried to fool the Phoenix defense. They faked a hand off to the running back and tossed the ball to a wide receiver for a tricky end-around run. Most of the defense collapsed on the running back.

Not Tony.

58

Tony read the play, streaking toward the outside. He caught the receiver and tackled him for no gain.

The Knights had to settle for a field goal.

"Nice job, Mr. President," Nolan said to Tony as they crossed paths on the sideline.

"Thanks," Tony said. "Now it's your turn."

Nolan and the offense took the field. In the huddle, he addressed his teammates.

"This is it, guys. We're going to go heavy on the run game. Offensive line, you need to be beasts today. All right. Here we go."

As Nolan approached the line of scrimmage to call the signals, he took in the linebackers looking at him hungrily. They looked huge.

On the first play, Nolan handed off to T.J. for a run up the middle. The offensive line blasted a hole open that gave T.J. room to charge ahead for 15 yards. It was a great start.

The next couple plays were also runs, but they didn't gain much. On third down and six, Coach Lewis called for a curl pass. It was the simplest pass play in the Phoenix playbook. But it was an important one for Nolan to pull off without making a mistake.

Nolan called out the signals. He took the snap and dropped back. He ducked a rushing defender and fired a strike to Caden. Caden made the grab and was quickly tackled, but it was enough yardage.

First down!

With that first pass out of the way, Nolan relaxed. The Phoenix offense marched down the field to the three-yard line. It took a few tries, but on third down, the line surged forward and T.J. was able to leap over the pile and into the end zone for the touchdown.

CHAPTER 10

PURSUING PERFECTION

Three minutes remained. The Phoenix trailed, 34-28. They had a third down with four yards to go at the Knights' 48-yard line.

Coach Lewis sent in the play. Nolan took the snap and dropped back. He looked to his right, where Caden was slashing toward the middle of the field. Nolan stepped up in the pocket and fired the ball. The throw was just behind Caden and bounced off his outstretched fingertips before falling to the ground.

It was fourth down.

Coach Lewis called time out. Nolan met him on the sideline.

"Do you think you can pin them back, Nolan?" Coach Lewis asked.

"No problem," Nolan said. "Think there's enough time to punt?"

"Yes," said Coach Lewis. "But we'd have to get a quick stop. Aim for the corner. Let's do it."

Nolan took the field again, but this time he lined up in the punter position. He was shocked at how much more comfortable he felt. It was his favorite part of the game.

Luis snapped the ball. Nolan stepped, dropped, and sent the ball flying high and deep. The return man decided to let it bounce.

That was a mistake.

The ball landed on the two-yard line and bounced straight up. By the time it came down, one of the Phoenix punting team members was there to catch it. Nolan passed by Tony as the defense took the field.

"Nice punt," Tony said.

"Thanks," Nolan said. "Get the ball back!"

Three plays in a row, the Knights ran the ball. Each time they did, the running back was gang-tackled at the line of scrimmage. They made no yards but burned a lot of time off the clock.

With less than a minute remaining, the Knights punted the ball back to the Phoenix. The return man called for a fair catch on the Knights' 40-yard line. They were still down by six points.

T.J. picked up a chunk of yardage on two straight rushes, but it was taking too much time. With 15 seconds left on the clock, the Phoenix tried a deep pass that fell incomplete. Five seconds remained. Coach Lewis called time out. The Phoenix were stuck at the Knights' 26-yard line. It was fourth down. There was time for just one last play.

Nolan knew the exact play for the moment: the flea flicker.

When he told Coach Lewis his plan on the sideline, Coach Lewis frowned. "Flea flicker? We've never practiced any such play."

"I practiced it with a few of the guys at the park," Nolan said. "Trust me, Coach. I think it could work."

Coach Lewis said, "Well, we don't have many other options. Let's do it."

"Thanks, Coach," said Nolan.

When Nolan called the flea flicker in the huddle, Caden flashed a big smile.

Nolan called out the signals and took the snap. He handed off to T.J., who charged ahead, stopped, and flipped the ball back to Nolan. The defense was crashing in hard. As a defensive tackle broke through, Nolan brought his arm back and rifled the ball as hard as he could. The ball soared in Caden's direction down the right sideline. The defensive tackle smashed into Nolan, knocking him to the turf.

For a second, Nolan couldn't breathe. Then, as the defensive tackle got off of him, the air whooshed back into his lungs. He heard the sound of the whistle blowing and a loud groan from the Knights' home crowd. He also heard a cheer go up from his own sideline.

When he got to his feet, he saw Caden standing in the end zone with the ball held high. The referee threw his hands into the air, signaling the touchdown. The Phoenix had done it!

Nolan's teammates swarmed him. Surprisingly, Tony was one of the first ones at Nolan's side.

"Nice throw!" Tony said. "You really took a hit."

"Thanks," Nolan said.

"You're a good punter and a decent quarterback," Tony said. "Maybe you'd be a decent vice president, too?"

"You're asking me to be your vice?" said Nolan. "Really?"

Tony smiled, which was a strange look for Tony, Nolan thought. Tony stuck out his hand to shake on it.

Nolan shook Tony's hand, smiled back, and said, "It's a deal."

AUTHOR BIO

Tyler Omoth grew up in the small town of Spring Grove, Minnesota. He has written more than forty books for young readers as well as a few award-winning short stories. Tyler loves watching sports, particularly baseball, and getting outside for fun in the sunshine. He lives in sunny Brandon, Florida, with his wife, Mary, and feisty cat, Josie.

ILLUSTRATOR BIO

Sean Tiffany has worked in the illustration and comic book field for more than twenty years. He has illustrated more than sixty children's books for Capstone and has been an instructor at the famed Joe Kubert School in northern New Jersey. Raised on a small island off the coast of Maine, Sean now resides in Boulder, Colorado, with his wife, Monika, their son, James, a cactus named Jim, and a room full of entirely too many guitars.

GLOSSARY

auditorium—the part of a public building where an audience sits

beckon—to summon or signal, typically with a wave or nod

campaign manager—an individual whose role is to coordinate the operations of a political campaign

enlist—to secure the support and aid of

formation—the way in which members of a group are arranged

long snapper—a center whose duty it is to hike the football for punts and placekicking attempts

second-string—a substitute player, not a starter

special teams—a squad that is used for kickoffs, punts, or other special plays

DISCUSSION QUESTIONS

1. Nolan loves being a punter, even though some of his teammates didn't respect the position. Is there a position in any team sport that you really like, even though it's not the most popular?

2. Caden helps Nolan to learn the quarterback position. If you knew how to play a position, would you help your teammate learn it even if you wanted the position for yourself?

3. Nolan runs for class president, but ends up losing the election to Tony. Were you surprised when Tony asked Nolan to be his vice president? Why do you think Nolan says yes?

WRITING PROMPTS

1. Write a short scene where Nolan teaches Caden how to launch the perfect punt.

2. Rewrite the last scene, but this time, make Nolan the winner of the class president election. How does he react to Tony? Remember, he's already asked Luis to be his V.P.

3. Write a poem about football. It can be about one position, the whole game, or your favorite part to watch. Use the words spiral, turf, touchdown, and handoff.